The JUNGLE in My Yard

By Jo Cleland

Illustrated by Anita DuFalla

"Mom, what's a jungle?" I ask.
"A place where animals live,"
she says.

4

5

I go to my back yard.

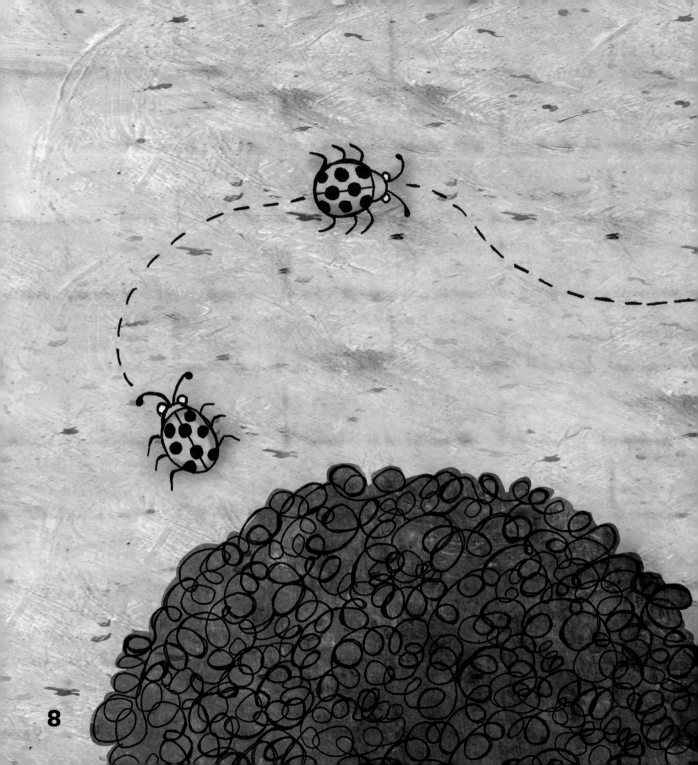

8

I see a bug on the wall.
I watch it crawl.

9

I see a squirrel on the ground with a nut it found.

I see a frog hop by chasing a fly.

I see a cat and rat.
Off they scat!

My dog jumps up. I love my pup!

I go back inside.

"Where have you been?"
Mom asks.

20

After Reading Activities

You and the Story...

Have you ever pretended you were in the jungle?

What animals would you see in the jungle?

Have you ever been to the zoo? Have you seen some of the jungle animals in the zoo?

Words You Know Now...

Each word is missing a vowel. Can you write the words on a piece of paper and add the missing vowel.

an_mals	j_ngle
ch_sing	sc_t
cr_wl	squ_rrel
gr_und	w_tch
ins_de	

You Could... Pretend Your Yard or the Park Is a Jungle

- What animals will be in your jungle?

- Draw a picture of the animals in your jungle.

- Label the animals in your picture.

- What is your favorite animal in your jungle?

About the Author

Jo Cleland enjoys writing books, composing songs, and making games. She lives in Arizona so the animals in her yard are lizards, coyotes, and javelinas.

About the Illustrator

Acclaimed for its versatility in style, Anita DuFalla's work has appeared in many educational books, newspaper articles, and business advertisements and on numerous posters, book and magazine covers, and even giftwraps. Anita's passion for pattern is evident in both her artwork and her collection of 400 patterned tights. She lives in the Friendship neighborhood of Pittsburgh, Pennsylvania with her son, Lucas.